Rebecka

by FRANK ASCH

Harper & Row, Publishers
New York, Evanston, San Francisco, London

FOR CONNIE

Rebecka is my dog,
and I'm her boy.

While I'm at school
Rebecka sits in the backyard
with no one to play with.

When I come home
she's so happy
she jumps all over me,

and we play together
all day long.

Yesterday, a girl moved in next door.

She wanted to know
if I wanted to play house
with her.

But I told her
I was already married.

"Her name is Rebecka.
You must come over
and visit us sometime."

Later, I thought—
"Wouldn't it be nice
  if I *could* marry Rebecka.

"Wouldn't it be nice
   to go on a honeymoon together
   around the world,

"and live in
her doghouse!

"But I wonder
  what we would eat…

"and what would our kids
be like!"

Today, the girl from next door
came over
and asked to meet
my wife.

So I took her out
to Rebecka's doghouse
and explained.

"She's not really my wife.
But she's my dog,
and I'm her boy."

All day
we played house together.

 I was the daddy,
 the girl from next door
 was the mommy,
 and Rebecka was the dog.

727374759876554321

Harper & Row, Publishers, Inc.
Published simultaneously in Canada by Fitzhenry & Whiteside Limited, Toronto.
Library of Congress Catalog Card Number: 72-76522
Trade Standard Book Number: 06-020149-S
Harpercrest Standard Book Number: 06-020150-9
FIRST EDITION